CAYE BOY

"caye" sounds like "key" and means "island"

BY JESSICA RETSECK WIGH   ILLUSTRATED BY ANDREW YOUNG

For Brad and our Caye Boys. And for all the island children who have played
under and around (and around and around) our house. -JRW

For Mom, Bridget and Audrey. -AY

I'm GILFORD.

I live in a little blue house,
on a little island,
in the middle of a GREAT BIG sea.

My house sits HIGH up on stilts to catch a breeze. It has a big porch with hammocks and lots of space to play and chase my little brother around.

My island
is a little
swoop of sand
with fish
and boats
all around it.

It is full of bright houses
and pretty flowers
and about a hundred coconut trees.

I can WALK and WALK and WALK and always end up back at my little blue house.

As soon as the sun wakes up, Alvis and I run into Mama and Pa's room.

"The sun is up! We're AWAKE!" we shout.

Mama says we are worse than a couple of roosters.

Then Alvis
and I romp and
stomp around the
porch until Mama finally
says we can go outside.

"Try not to wake up the whole island," calls Mama.
"And stay in the YARD!"

A "yard"
means "not-in-the-middle-of-the-street,"

So,
we stay in our yard
until we get to the beach,
which isn't our yard,
but is not-in-the-middle-of-the-street either,
so it counts.

We are GOOD listeners.

We have about a hundred hermit crab races, which takes FOREVER because hermit crabs aren't straight walkers.

I couldn't find my best hermit crab today.

His name is Hermes. He is the FASTEST crab on my island.

He wears a white plastic lid instead of a shell.

Mama says that is UNUSUAL.

Alvis finds
two empty bottles.
He's a good finder!

So, we wait,
and wait,
and wait,

until Miss Juanita FINALLY opens the store.

We trade the bottles for two shillings and we are RICH.

Then we trade our shillings for two bags of chips and that is even better.

Alvis and I race to catch up with our
friend Dario on his way to school.
His Pa always gives us a mango
from his fruit cart.

Mama says we have to eat lots
of good-for-us-food to grow
into BIG BOYS...

...so we tell her about the mangos
but not about the chips.

We like to help out at our cousin's snorkel shop. Alvis shows everyone how to put on flippers.

Tourists smell like sunscreen and ALWAYS ask us about a hundred questions.

I help Big George carry the long pole for his manatee tour because it is SO heavy.

I am a good helper.

I tell the tourists about all the fish they will see.
My best fish is the Spotted Drum.
    And the Angelfish.
    And the Queen Triggerfish.
    And about a hundred more kinds.

Snorkeling is the VERY best thing in the whole world.

We see Pa's boat come in so we ride to the dock to see what he caught.

Pa used to be a CAYE BOY like me, but then he grew BIG and now he is a fisherman.

Pa gives us some fish scraps to feed the frigates.

They swoop down and don't quite touch us, but ALMOST!

After lunch, I have to be quiet as a gecko because all the babies and big people take naps.

The sun is HOT, HOT, HOT, so I keep under houses mostly.

I practice crawling under Mr. Rodolfo's hammock without making a peep...

...pick some coco plums...

...see how close I can get to an iguana...

...lay under our water vat and spy on the chickens...

...and win my best marble back from Julio.

Since Mama isn't around to tell me to COME-DOWN-RIGHT-NOW, I climb the breadfruit tree. It is my best tree.

I can see my WHOLE island from the top.

Finally,
  after a hundred years,
  everyone wakes up
  from their naps
  and I can whoop around and
  make as MUCH noise as I want.

All the big kids come home from school, so we race
and chase each other until we are SO tired we crash
down and make sand angels.

Then comes the BEST time of day...lobstering time!

Pa swims around and uses a big hook to scoop up the lobsters. That is the EASY part. I have to make sure they don't scramble out of the bag, which everyone knows is the HARD part.

I'm a good lobsterman.

While Pa cleans the lobster, I go get an orange juice with Mama and Alvis.

We wait at Horse Eye Jack's. That is where everyone on the island goes to drink juice and laugh and swim.

The tourists always take HUNDREDS of pictures of the sun going down into the sea.

The sun gets bigger and bigger and lower and lower

and then it goes away and it is NIGHTTIME.

Pa rides us back to my little blue house.

Mama and Alvis
are cuddling in one
of the hammocks,
so Pa and I climb
into the other one.

My island is cool
and dark and quiet.

"The sun is down," I say. "It is tired."
"Yes, the sun is sleeping," says Pa.

"When will the sun wake up?" I ask.
"When YOU wake up," says Pa.

THE END

Made in the USA
San Bernardino, CA
06 March 2015